CATCHING BUTTERFLIES

Uba Franklin

Publishers:
Christmas Film Books
13 Suleimon Odufuwa Street
Ikorodu, Lagos, Nigeria
(+234)-8034557563
cristmasfilmbooks@gmail.com

DEDICATION

For

Oluoma & Adaeze

CONTENTS

PUBLISHERS PREFACE

Young people in Africa have a story to tell the world. And for long their voices have not been heard. As the economy of our continent soars up and plummets down on economic matrices beyond the capacities of our largely self-imposed leaders, so also does the quality and quantity of literature that is accessible to our youths in libraries and bookshops.

As a response, the Christmas book series has been conceived to plug this void on a digital level. Our books speak to the youths of Africa, arousing curiosity and provokes nostalgia; hopefully, it will be enjoyed by a wide spectrum of people globally.

Today we are proud to bring before you a story that will surprise and inspire many.

Enjoy.

PROLOGUE

August 1996.

The cream blue 504 Airport taxi was making close to 180 *kph* on the road to Zaria. It was drizzling lightly that August morning and the asphalt glistened as the car zipped through time. Traffic was light and the broad fast lane indulged speed.

Kano… this was her first time in the ancient city of Kano and the atmosphere that greeted Lile on arrival at the Kano International Airport was quite an anti-climax to all her expectations.

She might as well have been in Lagos with its cacophony of touts, beggars and harassed travellers.

Lile Yusuf sighed to herself and reclined in the back of the taxi, alone and cosy in the warmth of the car, Lile had her thought miles away in Zaria with Ibrahim, her boyfriend. Tomorrow will mark another birthday for Lile and on the spur of the moment she had packed up her small travelling bag and headed for the local airport; she had travelled all the way from Lagos this morning on the first flight out of the city just to pay Ibrahim a surprise visit.

Lile smiled with anticipation. Ibrahim would be astonished. Only yesterday he had called to discuss their future plans together and had wished Lile a lovely birthday outing with her schoolmates, he said he wished she was in Zaria to share her birthday with him. Lile smiled in the taxi, her face glowing and softened by memories of Ibrahim Dambaba.

From her handbag, Lile brought out a piece of paper to jot down the gifts and list of shopping items she intended to purchase once in Zaria with Ibrahim.

First, she would have to convert some dollars to naira but Ibrahim would know the best place.

For a long time, Lile was silent and contemplative as she made up a list of things to buy and then she brought out an initial sum of five hundred and fifty dollars and kept this and the list in her shirt pocket. That should fetch at least N50,000 in the black market.

Suddenly the car started losing speed and Lile was pulled back to the present.

A tollgate was approaching and the driver wound down his side window to pay the toll fee.

The car was immediately crowded with hawkers plying their wares in the rain. From bread to compact discs, they sold everything and were pushing at the window to catch madam's attention.

Looking at them in the drizzling rain trying to etch out a meagre living, Lile felt a wash of pity for them. As the taxi pulled away some of them futilely ran some steps after the car.

The driver wound up his window and the warmth returned while *Celine Dione's* mellow voice lulled Lile to sleep.

Ibrahim would be happy to see her but Daddy would be mad, especially as she had travelled to Kano without informing him. In fact, she'd told no one she was coming to Zaria, not even her roommate Maureen at Lagos State University. Lile smiled drowsily; what was the use of a surprise visit if she could not keep it a secret.

Lile Yusuf wanted her twenty- second birthday to be special and above all to spend it together with Ibrahim Dambaba. Daddy would just have to understand and pardon her again… and again! Lile smiled to herself, feeling naughty and happy as she drifted off to sleep…

* * * * * *

The screeching of tires on slippery tarmac startled Lile from sleep and for one unbelieving moment, it was as though everything was happening in slow-motion, from one frame to another frame of inexorable fate on a film editor's timeline.

At 160 *kph* the driver had negotiated a sharp bend right into a crossing herd of Fulani cattle. A sharp swerve and the tires lost traction on the wet road, skidded and spun out of control. Suddenly the car jumped and flipped out of the road. Metal and glass exploded everywhere as the 504 crashed into a boulder and caught fire. And then a terrible explosion; flames engulfed the car and the dying scream of the driver caught between the dashboard.

For Lile, it was strange unreality. Her bleeding body lay sprawled on the road where she had been thrown out of the somersaulting car. Three cows lay struggling in death near her and people were shouting hysterically around her, yet she couldn't move, couldn't talk, totally paralysed, and she felt consciousness receding gradually from her like one who is falling down weightless from the sky.

Lile Yusuf felt a peculiar rushing buoyancy taking hold of her mind. Over and over her mind kept re-running a phrase from her recent dream like a broken record, sound of Ibrahim Dambaba's laughter and astonishment as he swung her round and round in his arms, *"Lile, baby you're totally crazy; you flew all the way from Lagos to hear happy birthday!"*

And the sound of his laughter echoing over and over and over again in her mind, Ibrahim Dambaba and Lile Yusuf....

CHAPTER ONE

Allen Close in Dolphin Heights Estate belonged to the class of multi-billionaire residents.

The Close was home to oil and power barons, retired army generals, blue-chip industrialists, bank owners, political heavyweights and drug merchants, even questionable tycoons and many business men and women.

The houses at Allen Close are beyond believe in terms of grandeur and sheer opulence. Each house exuded an aura of awe and arrogance, invoking a sense of intimidation and magnitude on first-time visitors.

Maureen stood hesitantly in front of the massive designer gate of house No.3, trying to summon up the courage to ring the bell.

She had come to the house once before in the company of Lile Yusuf about three years ago. The General was still serving in the army then and was away on a mission abroad. Maureen still vividly recalled her awe and amazement on discovering that Lile, with all her humility and friendliness in school, belonged to a mansion like this.

"You mean this is really your home, Lile? Are you sure!"

And Lile grinned had grinned at Maureen's dismay.

10

"It's no big deal, Maureen. In fact, it's boring. Most times I live here all alone, except when Daddy's in the country. It's a big boring and lonely house... just like a beautiful prison"

That was three years ago.

Maureen took a deep breath to calm herself and she reached up and depressed the bell and waited. Almost at once a side door by the gate opened and, apparently, the gateman stared quizzically at Maureen.

In corrupt English, "Who you *dey* find here?"

"Hello, my name's Maureen - Maureen Ojo. I'm Lile's friend... we're roommates at *Lagos State University*. Please is Lile at home?"

The gateman smiled at her and looked less hostile now. "Ah, Lile never come home today o, she tell you say she *dey* come house today?"

Maureen shook her head and looked rather perplexed.

"Look, I've not seen Lile for the past ten days. She has missed two important tests in school. I thought perhaps she was sick at home, that's why I came here to see her."

"I no understand you, madam, you mean to say Lile no *dey* school for the past ten days? Where she come go now?"

"I don't know, she told me she wanted to go home for two days and celebrate her birthday and come back and prepare for her tests. It's ten days now and she's not yet back."

The gateman scratched his head and looked dumbfounded.

"*Abegi* this your talk *don* pass my power, make you come inside come see her papa...."

This invitation totally alarms Maureen. The prospect of meeting Lile's dad alone really unnerved her.

"The General is around!"

"Yes."

"Can't you... can't you deliver the message...?"

Maureen sounded a bit frightened at the prospect of meeting Lile's father.

"I don't know *wetin* I go tell General o, this story pass my power, make you come and explain to him yourself madam."

Maureen reluctantly followed the gateman inside the compound.

Stepping into the compound, once again she felt an overpowering sense of awe as she looked around the compound.

The lawns and hedges around the drive were a lush green and trimmed. An assortment of flowering plants and royal palms thronged the compound. The mansion towered up in front of her, an edifice of marble, glass and oak doors.

In front of the foyer, a powerful, shining metallic grey E-class gleamed in the morning sunlight. Six other Jeeps and luxury rides lined an open garage on the left flank of the mansion.

They mounted a short flight of stairs and the gateman beckoned her inside the Living room.

"Make you sit down here for children parlour until *Oga* come down from upstairs. He get some work he *dey* do."

With that, the gateman left Maureen to herself and walked back to his post.

Maureen looked around. The children parlour was heavily rugged in burgundy. Two Ac's hummed silently. Huge upholstered chairs in the same wine-red colour claimed pride of position in front of the electronic cabinet, and heavy blinds draped the room.

The lighting was quite muted, soft and deliberately positioned to enhance the effects of several large framed paintings of wildlife and mountains and snowcapped peaks....

Maureen sank gratefully into a comfortable chair and waited for the presence of the General. Besides her on a side table was a crystal ashtray crafted in the shape of a tortoise.

Maureen picked it up and surveyed this piece of art. It caught the ray of sunlight streaming in from a window behind Maureen and scattered fine colours like a prism.

"Wonderful".

Maureen smiled.

She kept back the ashtray.

"Do you like it?"

A heavy baritone voice.

Maureen spun around in fresh alarm and the old man laughed pleasantly as he came down the flight of stairs towards Maureen and offered his hand for a handshake.

"You must be Maureen, Lile's friend. Sule called from the gate to tell me you were waiting for me. So how are you, young lady? I'm Lile's father."

The General was a tall man, dark complexioned and lean with a slight paunch. His hair was greying rapidly and Maureen guessed his age to be somewhere in the late fifties or early sixties. He grasped her hand firmly in his large hand and his brown eyes fixed penetratingly on her own. Just like his daughter, he had eyes the colour of fresh honey.

Maureen found herself looking at the floor shyly with unexplainable embarrassment. This old man exuded a disturbing potency around him like a magnetic spell.

The General took a sit and claimed a cell phone on his side stool and dialled a number expertly with one hand while he lit a cigarette at the same time.

"So do you like my ashtray?" he asked Maureen again and chucked, "I caught you examining one."

"They are fine, thank you, Sir," Maureen said softly, thanking him for no reason.

"China; I got them last year in China while there on business". He tapped ashes into one for emphasis and without pause, he was on a different topic entirely.

"How old are you?"

"Sir?"

"I said - oh never mind, my call is through…"

For several minutes he spoke into the phone in Hausa and Maureen took this opportunity to casually examined him.

General M.S Yusuf was an old man but he did not share the effeminate softness of old men. The General was hard and rugged and the only weakness about him seemed to be his paunch. He had a deep baritone voice and an open, amiable feature.

Looking at him without appearing to be doing so Maureen instantly felt attracted to him and at the same time, she felt a certain dread. This man lost his wife over twenty years ago and since then had not deemed it necessary to remarry.

The General finished his call and clicked shut the cellular phone and dropped this in the breast pocket of his suit. His manner had become quite abrupt.

"So Maureen what can I do for you, my dear?"

"Sir, I haven't seen Lile for the past ten days now. She has missed two tests so far in school. I came to find out if maybe she was sick or something…" Maureen's soft voice tapered of helplessly.

Major General M.S Yusuf. (Retired) was a man of considerable force and arrogance. He was an extremely successful career soldier and now retired, he had built an intimidating fortune in the oil sector. His rivals called him a cunning fox, a cold and ruthless man. General M.S Yusuf executed business and politics with the same military strategy and precision he would employ in a war theatre. He was an astute gambler and would readily stake the lives of his men, his reputation and his money to achieve whatsoever he sought.

But over the years, especially these last couple of years, General MS Yusuf had come to love his daughter. And he had gone about winning her love and respect with the same single-minded intensity he had employed to become the successful man he had become in his business and military career.

In the end of the day, his daughter was all that he had left, all that really mattered. And no one knew that now better than the General.

General M.S Yusuf had lost his son and his beautiful wife at childbirth twenty years ago and his bloody career had not given him the time to remarry. And now, almost too late, he decided to claim the love of his daughter and heir, Lile Yusuf.

And now this.

The General sat very still and silent, cat eyes fixed on Maureen and the young girl felt like a butterfly pinned to the upholstered chair.

16

Maureen said brokenly, "I'm really confused. All Lile told me was that she wanted two days break from school to spend her birthday at home. So I actually thought she was coming here but..." Maureen shrugged unhappily, "I'm sorry sir, but I don't know what else to say. Maybe she travelled to Zaria, to see Ibrahim"

"Maybe," said the old man softly, "maybe...."

Once more he reached for his cellular phone and slowly crushed his cigarette in a crystal ashtray.

CHAPTER TWO

The tall looking young girl sat in a wheelchair under the shade of a mango tree, engrossed in the content of a magazine.

Her head was heavily bandaged and her left leg was still in a white plaster cast, stretched out in front of her. She was a courageous girl and her easy acceptance of her fate had already won her many friends at the Kano-based Intensive Care Hospital.

Watching this girl from a window in the doctor's office Mrs Adams felt a lot of compassion for the girl's plight.

"Her name is Lile," Doctor Bala informed the woman. "And that is all she can recall about herself. Just that one name, Lile."

"It sounds all so horrible," Mrs Adams said.

"Acute amnesia. The trauma to her head was severe, almost fatal. When those unknown men dumped her in front of our gate we thought she was dead. It's a miracle that she's still alive. A wonderful miracle."

Doctor Bala, a smallish looking prescription-glass wearing dark skinned man with balding and greying hair owned Intensive Care Hospital. Again he found himself

18

recounting to Mrs Adams the events of that fateful day three weeks ago when some unknown men had stopped their pickup truck in front of his hospital and forcefully discarded the unconscious body of Lile on his hapless security guard. She was left there in a pool of her blood and the guard had been forced to rush her inside the hospital.

Dr Bala said, "I was scared because she was almost dead, hardly breathing, and I didn't want the added *wahala* and complications with her people and the police if anything happened to her under my watch.

"However, I couldn't just sit there and watch her die. Such a young, healthy and beautiful girl. So we transferred her to the theatre and searched her clothes for identification papers. Guess what we found inside her shirt pocket, madam?"

"What?"

"Nothing! Just a shopping list… and five hundred and fifty dollars!"

"Oh my goodness!" Mrs Adams was quite astonished. "Five hundred and fifty dollars! That's a lot of money!"

"Yes, we found that much money on her. And that made me realise the girl hadn't been a crime victim as we had first assumed. She is probably an accident victim, and the men who dumped her on us were probably good Samaritans who didn't want to get more involved than they could help."

"I understand. The police can be very obnoxious in such cases."

Mrs Adams stared at the girl. Even from that distance Mrs Adam's could see she was a pretty, young thing.

"She's been here three weeks you say, and nobody has asked after her?"

Dr Bala nods his head.

"Her family probably don't even know her whereabouts and obviously they haven't noticed her absence from home...."

"Negligence," said Dr Bala, "it's a classical rich kid-rich parent relationship."

"Not my Ronke!" retorted Mrs Adams with some vehemence. "Ronke is everything to Dele and I."

Dr Bala chuckled, "Oh you're different, Mrs Adams. It was silly of me to make such a blanket statement like that just now. Besides, Ronke is an only child and an anaemic patient to boot. As her mum, you and Ronke are bound to be strongly bonded. She is everything to you.

"But believe me, most rich parents are too busy making money these days to give proper time for family bonding. They think that throwing money at their kids and indulging them with expensive habits is enough compensation for their busy schedule. It's clearly not enough, Mrs Adams, they're destroying these kid. And no matter how hard they try, money cannot replace a relationship."

Looking at the girl through the window in Dr Bala's office Mrs Adams wondered what was going through the mind of the young girl.

"She's only a baby."

* * * * * *

Lile looked up from her magazine as the elderly woman approached her. The woman looked kind-faced and motherly, dark in complexion and on the bulky side. She sat down on a bench beside Lile's wheelchair and introduced herself.

"I am Mrs Adams. This is our family hospital. My Ronke is having her periodic checkup, she's a sickle cell patient and she suffered a crisis recently."

"I'm so sorry to hear that." Lile returned the magazine to her lap with some pain. "I hope she's feeling better now?"

"Oh, she is, poor baby. She is so brave about the whole thing. And to think she's suffering so much because her parents were too selfish, too preoccupied with ourselves to care about medical consequences."

Lile shakes her head gently, "Don't blame yourself, Mummy."

The woman smiled. "Well, we're paying the price for our self-centeredness. Besides, we haven't dared raise another child for sheer dread…

"But enough of me; I came here to talk about you. Dr Bala has just been telling me your case history. Is it true you don't remember anything about yourself or…" and Mrs Adams lowered her voice conspiratorially, "you're only acting that you don't remember anything, like in the movies?"

Lile could not help laughing and Mrs Adams saw that she really was beautiful in a subtle, charming manner. She had an oval, nomadic face dimpled on both cheeks when she smiled. She was a tall girl, slim and mild complexioned but the striking thing about her were her eyes, they were light gold, the colour of fresh African honey and sparkled with her laughter.

Her voice was soft and pleasant with a faintly northern, almost untraceable well-schooled accent. Mrs Adams easily zeroed her for a Fulani girl.

"I really wish I was faking amnesia, Mrs Adams. Each time I try to think I end up with a splitting headache". Lile lightly touched her bandaged head softly. "Everything is blank upstairs. I don't even know how I know that I am called Lile. I just feel that's my name."

"Poor little child," Mrs Adams was clearly touched. "And please, I like it when you call me mummy."

"Everybody has been so nice to me here. The nurses, the doctors, everybody. Even the patients here are very nice to me."

"That's because you radiate sunshine. Look at me, an hour ago I did not know you, but now I feel I know a lot about you."

Lile smiled teasingly.

"Maybe you can tell me who I am then, Mummy. Whether I have a father and mother, a Christian or a Muslim, whether I am Ibo, Hausa or Yoruba or Idoma - whether I am married or single, just little details thing like that". Her voice hung in the air, sad and plaintive.

Mrs Adams took her hand. "Look, child, don't think of these things now. Don't force yourself to think about all these painful and, for now, clearly irrelevant things. Just concentrate on getting well and slowly your memory with come back.

"I was talking to Dr Bala some minutes ago about you and he said you have been very traumatised, probably in a ghastly motor accident. He said you were in a coma for almost four days! Four days! They had to shave your head and operated on you three times." Mrs Adams held her eyes warmly. "Lile, it is a miracle that you are alive, just be grateful to God."

Tears were spilling down the Lile's face by now. Mrs Adams helped her to wipe her tears.

"Be strong, Lile. Don't give in to despair. You will overcome these challenges step by step. These are the same words I tell my baby."

* * * * * *

Doctor Bala worked late into the night in his office trying to analyse the new bits of information from Mrs Adams talk with Lile. The young girl was an enigma, one whose mystery was becoming an obsession with Doctor Bala.

I have been in this profession for thirty-two years, Dr Bala thought, and I have never come across a case like this one before. The girl was a total blank as to her own history and as she recovered and gained strength physically she would also become increasingly worried and emotionally distressed, and if left uncontained may her distress could easily snowball into full fledge hysteria unless Dr Bala could provide answers for Lile.

It was often the case with Amnesiacs. And in Lile's peculiar case it was worse because nobody had yet shown up to claim and re-orient her. Even the police had not shown up again after the initial questioning when the case had been reported to them by Dr Bala. They were probably content with the fact that the girl was safe in Dr Bala's hands.

Dr Bala was a small man in stature but with considerable intellect and initiative. He presided over four other doctors and interns that worked for him. For twenty years he had almost single-handedly built up the Intensive Care Hospital to its present reputation of excellence and an exalted list of wealthy client attested to his overwhelming success.

This was probably the reason why Doctor Bala had risked the challenge of Lile's case where other less determined practitioners would have baulked or felt incapacitated and reluctant to handle an unknown and dying accident victim.

They had quickly transferred the unconscious girl to a life-support machine while an assay of her blood had been quickly carried out. Some bones were fractured and she was bleeding internally but thankfully she showed a normal blood glucose level. She would survive.

Now, three weeks later, Dr Bala sat late in his office examining his file and the scanty identity profile he had drawn up for Lile:

01.   *Name:*   *Lile*
02.   *Language:*   *Multilingual*
03.   *Age Estimate:*   *22± 2yrs*
04.   *Height:*   *5' 10"*
05.   *Sex:*   *Female*
06.   *Blood Group:*   *AB*

07.	Eye colour:	Light brown
08.	Facial Mark:	None
09.	Ibrahim:	Father, husband, brother, boyfriend?
10.	Lagos, Abuja:	Familiar towns to Lile, (Why not Kano?)
11.	Possession:	Shopping-list, $550, Elizabeth Arden designer wristwatch, a golden neck chain with a butterfly pendant. Expensive leather Jacket and Tee-shirt, Lee jeans and sneakers.

Examining the last entry Dr Bala found himself wondering about the pendant. If only it had been a cross, that would at least have solved one small part of her mystery.

That Lile came from a wealthy home was quite evident and Dr Bala did not worry about the eventual settlement of his medical bill - that was secondary to the driving curiosity he had for unraveling her enigma. For him the girl was a piece of *DNA* helix and the key to reading her coded mystery was somewhere in her head, embedded deep within her dark subconscious mind.

"Who are you, Lile?" Dr Bala asked of her file, "who are you Lile? Talk to me, talk to me, talk to me...."

CHAPTER THREE

T he head office of Oiltech Industrial Services firm was situated in a multi-story building off the Agidingbi Industrial hub, Ikeja, Lagos. The company occupied the entire third floor of the building. The oil company also had three other branches in Abuja, Warri and Port Harcourt.

Major General M.S. Yusuf owned Oiltech. The company served as the arrowhead of his several business concerns and with it, he had bulldozed his way as an active player in the vital oil and gas sector of the country. The oil firm was not yet three years old but already it had a commanding presence among major oil servicing companies in the country. Thanks to a powerful cabal of 'oldboy' networks and the practical hijack of the oil sector by the military institution from civilians in the last 40 years of military dictatorship in Nigeria. In fact, there is hardly any oil company, servicing or producing, that is not heavily polluted by a permissive military presence. Retired or serving, the Generals owned the vital oil sector of Nigeria.

Ibrahim Dambaba's blue five series *BMW* was well known to the gatemen at the Oiltech premises and the guards let him drive in after a brief exchange of pleasantries. Ibrahim was a regular visitor and the staffs of the company liked him. Behind his back, they referred to him fondly as "our in-law."

Above, the sky was overcast and dull, pregnant with rain clouds. Ibrahim packed and locked his car and strode into the building. He chose to mount the stairs rather than wait for the lift.

At twenty-nine, Ibrahim was tall of stature and fair of complexion, athletic looking. He had graduated four years ago from ABU with a degree in Business Administration, and after the compulsory one-year National Service, he was made a manager in one of his uncle's companies.

However, two years ago he had easily secured a study leave from the company and enrolled as a student pilot at the *Nigeria College of Aviation Technology (NCAT), Zaria*. This was in fulfilment of a childhood dream of his to become a pilot like one of his favourite maternal uncle.

This was Ibrahim's third visit to Oiltech to see Lile's old man in the past two weeks. Also, he had been to the house several times, sometimes in the company of his father, Rear Admiral Shehu Dambaba of the Nigerian Navy.

The two families went way back to their roots in Niger State. Admiral Dambaba and M.S Yusuf had known each other even before their army days. The two had joined the military at about the same time but had been drawn to different arms of the military. They had been mates at the *NMC* and later, Jaji.

They had profited enormously from the IBB years and in the military circle had been part of the cardinal caucus obliquely referred to as the Minna Mafia.

However, with the forced ascendancy of the Iron General, the man with the dark goggles, the Minna group had lost out somewhat in the power equation and only recently did they regain their former prestige and influence with the enthronement of one of their own as the incumbent C-in-C, the dark and amiable General Adbulsalami Abubakar.

The General's P.A. politely informed Ibrahim that General M.S Yusuf was with the commissioner of police and asked him to wait. Ibrahim picked up a magazine and sat down in a divan beside the commissioner's police orderly. Two very important looking businessmen were waiting for the General and Ibrahim exchanged pleasantries with them in Hausa. They asked after his dad.

Ibrahim tried to read.

The *TELL* magazine he had chosen was the latest issue and irritatingly they were still eulogising Abiola several months after the man's death. It seemed as though all the Nigerian papers and TV stations had no other topic to write about except about MKO Abiola, his life and many achievements, and eventually his very high profile death before the eyes of the world.

Ibrahim was indifferent to *MKO* Abiola as a person; he was clearly a great and powerful man, in fact, a business icon. However, he posed too great a danger to a cabalistic order that existed long before he was conceived and *insha Allah*, would continue to prevail in Nigeria.

To Ibrahim and most of his northern friends, Abiola became who he was because he rode on the shoulder of this feudal, conservative system only for him to turn around and fight a system that picked him up from the slum of life and ordained him a prince among his people. In the end, to Ibrahim, there was no loss in *MKO's* death as well as that of Abacha. They were simply two pawns in a chessboard and they had outlived their strategic relevance. Ibrahim felt no pity for either of these men. They were pawns who aspired to be kings in the chess board of life.

The inner door opened and the Lagos commissioner of police came out and the police orderly beside Ibrahim sprang up to full attention.

Ibrahim shook hands with the police boss. He had been to the man's office several times recently since Lile vanished. The commissioner shook hands with the other two Alhaji's who made their way together into the chairman's office.

Ibrahim quickly followed the commissioner to the lift, a bit anxious for good news.

"Any updates sir?"

The police boss shook his head negatively. "Sorry, Ibrahim. We are trying our best but information has been rather scarce. All the adverts on TV and on the newspapers have so far yielded nothing. The media and newspaper people are too distracted at the moment with Abacha, Abiola and the new regime. Nobody cares about the plight of one twenty-two-year-old girl, even if her father happens to be M.S. Yusuf.

"Right now we are working on the assumption that she has been kidnapped. So many people, especially these Niger-Delta hooligans, are holding silly grudges against Northerners in the oil sector."

Ibrahim stares unhappily at the police boss.

The policeman continued. "It is, however, puzzling to us that there has not been any ransom demand so far in this case. Anyway, we are really hoping that this is a case of ransom because then there is hope that she will be returned to us unharmed. To consider another alternative will be really tragic."

"One month is more than enough time for any stupid kidnapper to make their demand known," Ibrahim sounded truculent.

"That's true, but for now that's all we have to work on."

His lift arrived and the police boss shook hands again with Ibrahim.

"Don't worry, Ibrahim, we'll do our very best, *insha Allah.*"

The lift door closed and Ibrahim went back to his seat, annoyed and helpless. Stupid police people. They always had excuses for their incompetence. Why would Ogoni or Ijaw people come all the way to Lagos to kidnap a small girl when they had all those politically sensitive expatriate staffs working with Shell, Mobil and so many other Multinational oil companies in their Niger-Delta homeland. And since when did their Abacha problem become a general *northern* problem?

Oh, Lile, Lile, where are you? Ibrahim felt like killing all these sensation-minded news people who could not even spare a humanitarian article on a missing, innocent girl like Lile Yusuf. All they cared about was eulogising a man who practically poisoned himself when he turned around and bit the finger that had fed him fat on the land. And in a helpless show of frustration, Ibrahim flung the *TELL* magazine away from himself.

The General's pretty secretary showed no surprise. She got up and replaced the magazine properly.

Ibrahim felt ashamed. "I am sorry, madam," he apologised.

She smiled at him. "Don't worry too much Ibrahim. Lile will show up very soon, I am very certain of this. You'll see."

Ibrahim thanked her for her positive outlook and tried to relax. 11:45am. The air-conditioner was humming so soothingly and the tastefully furnished office was very pleasant to the eyes. Ibrahim was embarrassed to find his eyes swimming with tears. Quickly he turned his face and pretended he was wiping sweat from his face with a hanky.

* * * ** *

When Ibrahim got into the inner office, the General was standing in front of the ceiling-to-floor window, a glass of cognac in one hand and he was gazing intently at the street below, apparently oblivious to Ibrahim's presence. He was dressed expensively in flowing, blue babanriga.

"Sit down Ibrahim," the old man said in his deep baritone. "So good of you to come again."

Still he kept on gazing outside and after a while he said, "I am a good Muslim, Ibrahim. Why is this happening to me? I pray five times a day. I perform the yearly pilgrimage. I give alms conscientiously and I try very hard, Ibrahim, not to cheat my fellow men. Yes, I smoke, yes I drink, but even these little indulgences I am prepared to foreswear if Allah in his infinite mercy will bring back my daughter alive."

Ibrahim looked down at the cream rug. He didn't know how to respond to the pain of this man who kismet seemed bent on punishing in this very terrible and bizarre way.

The General collapsed tiredly on his chair, behind the large ornate table. The man looked tired and worn-out. These last few weeks had been pure torture. He had alerted the police, the *NSA,* the *DMI,* the *SSS, FRSC, NURTW,* who hadn't he notified? They had combed Lagos with a fine toothcomb. Nothing. Mortuaries, hospitals, hotels, schools, where hadn't they searched for her? Nothing. Finally, the search had been widened to include Abuja and Zaria. Still nothing. Six national dailies had carried her picture and twice the *NTA* had declared her missing. The entire private and independent radio and television houses in Lagos had declared her missing - Hajia Hauwawu Lile Yusuf. Nothing.

Three different-coloured desk phones sat serenely on the office table amidst a jumble of paper, books, trays, and personal paraphernalia yet out of habit M.S. Yusuf reached for his pocket cell phone and began to dial a number.

"Ibrahim, I am a tired old man," the General said as though he were crying inside.

Ibrahim maintained the silence. Lightning and thunder claimed the air, it soon began to rain.

CHAPTER FOUR

R onke Adams had suffered another major crisis and had been rushed to the Intensive Care Hospital. From the intensive unit ward, Ronke was later transferred on request to Lile's private ward so the two friends could always be together.

This convenient arrangement considerably lessened the pressure on Mrs Adams who could now afford to go home occasionally for that period of Ronke's hospitalisation.

Ronke Adams looked like a younger, tensed replica of her mother. Dark, average height and impulsive. At twenty two, she was underweight due largely to her ailment. She was a good looking girl, Ronke, with an open, generous face and she smiled easily, showing off her perfect gap-toothed allure. But Ronke's eyes held so much pain and the unrelenting agony of sickle cell anaemia seems to have stamped an indelible imprint on her personality.

"I have never known three months in my life without pain," she had told Lile in one of their many conversations. "I was born with pain as a gift... a dark gift."

Ronke lay propped in bed by several pillows; she was dressed in pyjamas and beside her lay Hugo, her big loving teddy bear.

For a long time, Ronke stared at Lile who was sleeping lightly in her own bed; her long plastered leg had dropped down beside the bed, resting on her wooden crutches. The bandage had been removed from Lile's head and her hair, that had been shaved during her operation, was growing back rapidly.

The time was past twelve in the night and the hospital was silent, the smell of medicine filled the air.

Watching her sleeping friend, Ronke felt compassion for the girl. Lile had been living in the hospital now for well over six weeks and yet she was no step nearer the solution to her unclaimed riddle. Nobody had shown up yet to place a tag on her.

Ronke knew that Lile worried a lot about this limbo-like situation although she hardly talked about herself. Who wouldn't worry? To wake up one day and find yourself all alone in the world with no history and medical bills piling higher every day.

Ronke looked at Hugo, lost in her private thoughts.

She must come home with me, Ronke decided suddenly and the decision felt so right, so wonderful and perfect that the girl wondered how come the thought had never occurred to herself or her thoughtful and pragmatic mother all this time.

Ronke shifted gently in bed and turned to hug her ever loyal teddy. "Hugo, I've found myself a sister."

* * * * * *

Next morning it was another lovely sun filled September morning and sunlight was pouring in through the drawn window blind into the little hospital room.

10:30 am.

The Doctor and nurses had already done their morning rounds, Ronke had gotten an extra injection and had more blood drawn from her arm for analysis.

The Doctor was one of the younger interns and after scribbling away on his chart and teasing the two girls, he departed with his nurses; a strong antiseptic fragrance trailed their exit.

Ronke made a face and flopped down on her bed with an exaggerated groan. "There's no question about it Lile, these people are selling my blood!"

Lile laughed pleasantly. The great thing about Ronke was the way she made light of her tragic condition. She had so much courage, Ronke Adams and looking at her, Lile felt empathy with her roommate.

The white of Ronke's eyes had turned a frightening, yellow hue, a side effect of the drugs she was being treated with, they were told. Still, Ronke would not be ambushed by self-pity. She employed laughter like a shield against despair.

Ronke turned serious.

"Lile, I have been discussing with Hugo about you. Hugo thinks it's time you came and lived with us until you are well enough to conquer this amnesia monster that has you imprisoned in an underground cell of your mind.

"Hugo promises to be a perfect gentleman and your guardian in our home. Hugo thinks six weeks in hospital is like an eternity in hell. Hugo really needs you."

Lile was touched. "Only if Dr Bala will permit me."

Ronke's eyes flashed yellow fire. "He dares not refuse any of my requests! He dares not!"

* * * * * *

Mrs Adams came in around eleven with their home cooked lunch. Osage came with her. Osage was Ronke's cousin and the two doted on each other.

Osage had been to the hospital several times before and already claimed he had a crush on Lile and openly confessed same to anybody who cared to listen. He was a jovial, easy-go-lucky sort of person. He was quite a dashing, energetic man, square-shouldered and average height. He worked with the Kano-based *Nitel* exchange department.

Osage knew a million and one jokes and the girls always looked forward to his visits. He came in with Mrs Adams and carried two large polyethene bags stocked full with a variety of fruits and Osage abruptly dumped one on each bed with emphasis.

"So how's mystery lady today?" he asked Lile.

"Osage, I didn't bring you here to come and disturb Lile," Mrs Adams scolded sternly only to defeat her cautioning by adding, "Have you recalled anything yet, darling?"

This had everybody laughing.

Lile said obligingly, "Last night I had a dream and in the dream, I saw this person and he seemed so familiar, like somebody I should know...."

Mrs Adams was instantly curious. "Can you describe what he looked like?"

"I have a fuzzy recollection at best, mummy," Lile said slowly, trying to recall the puzzling dream. "I know he's tall and dark and... and strong looking. I think he was dressed in an army uniform. I cannot... I can't really recollect how his face looked now but I remember calling him Daddy in the dream...."

For a while, after this, they were all silent. Then Mrs Adams broke the silence.

"Well never mind, darling. Everything will come back gradually. Now, both of you should eat."

"I'm already eating," Ronke laughed, peeling a banana. And to Osage with mock irritation, "Osage, for goodness sake, where are my lighthouse family CDs?'

Osage raised his hands in mutual banter. "Ronke, I promise you, I really promise you this time without failing, you'll have them tomorrow. Now can I have a banana?"

Ronke threw a bunch at him in exasperation.

* * * * * *

Mrs Adams and Osage were enthused by Ronke's proposal to Lile. Mrs Adams kept wondering why the idea had not crossed her mind since.

"To think I let you stay all these weeks in this cold and antiseptic prison when you could have been recuperating at our home. Oh, it's such a wonderful idea, girls!"

Lile smiled happily.

"I will introduce her to my world of computer paintings," Ronke informed her mother. "I know Lile will be ecstatic about my paintings. She has a rich mind; she will get me."

"I bet the poor girl will just be tortured for nothing and won't understands any of that bizarre stuff you call Art," Osage said this laconically and instantly drew Ronke's fire.

"She's not a thick skulled dullard like you, Osage. You know your problem, Mr Killjoy? You don't have the soul of a poet and it's eating you up. You have the soul of a tax collector!"

The women laughed gleefully and Osage protested hotly for Lile's benefit. "Don't mind her Lile, I love poetry, I love colours, I love music and arts – real arts. But Ronke's paintings are just a myriad of clashing colours and numbers and crazy shapes that only her can safely interpret.

"Ronke will tell you that this colour or that shape is the voice of a singing Angel - and who am I, a mere mortal - to argue the correlation between an Angel's voice and a crooked polygon?" Osage's hands were spread in amazement, which had everybody in mirth again.

Osage continued. "But let me be honest Lile, one good thing about your staying at Ronke's home, I promise I will help you locate your people wherever they are hiding in Kano. I know this town like the back of my hand. We will drive through every street, every nook and corner of Kano until we run into one of your people. That's a promise you can take to the bank!"

Osage sounded very sincere and Lile felt her hope rising.

"I am grateful, Osage."

Mrs Adams laughed. "Not too fast Lile. I know this young rascal very well. He probably has his own ulterior motives well worked out in advance of any philanthropy on his part. So be very careful with this wolf in sheep's clothing."

Once again Osage vigorously protested his innocent motive amidst their wicked laughter. Women!

CHAPTER FIVE

H ow time flew. Lile and Ronke were in Doctor Bala's office to say goodbye to the old man.

Ronke had been discharged that morning after being hospitalised for nine days but this time around it had not been so bad because she had had Lile to share the hours with her.

On her part, Lile was happy and guilty at the same time that she was about to leave the hospital. This morning she burst into tears when some of the nurses and doctors and patients crowded her small room to wish her goodbye. Some of them gave her little presents: novels, comics, cards, etcetera. Lile tried to say thank you but ended up crying instead.

In the medical director's office, the old doctor surveyed Lile with some pride.

"Look at you", he said, "just look at you, young Lady. You are a marvel of science, a living miracle. Nobody thought you would survive but here you are hale and hearty and, but for the limping leg, almost as physically fit as the proverbial fiddle."

"I can never quantify my gratitude, Doctor Bala," Lile said with a lot of feeling.

"Sir, what about her lost memory," Ronke asked. "How soon can Lile expect to regain her full memory?"

"That is a bit hard to say. You see, the human mind is an entirely mysterious and incomprehensible mechanism, absolutely dysfunctional when it suits it to be. In the case of amnesia, the mind shuts itself down to safeguard itself from excessive shock and trauma, like an electronic gadget would blow a fuse to safeguard itself from high voltage.

"However, and I say this with happy optimism, the wonderful thing about the mind is that it heals itself. All it needs is time.

"In Lile's case she sustained severe concussion and damage to the head - and generally such scale of physical abuse if survived can generate a threshold of shock so significant as to force the mind to blank out for a while.

"All Lile needs now is rest and avoidance of any sort of mental fatigue or emotional stress. Some people have been known to recover from amnesia within days and weeks, and then again some have known absolute or partial amnesia for months and even years."

"Years!" The two young girls gasped at this possibility.

Doctor Bala laughed to ease their anxiety.

"Easy now, Lile; don't fret. There are already very clear signs emerging to suggest that you will regain partial or even full memory soon enough. Like I said before, you need to rest yourself and I believe you will find that at the Adams' home.

"You see, the subconscious is like a computer and every single major or minor experience has been carefully recorded and classified inside here," Dr Bala tapped his forehead. "Nothing has been lost".

Again Lile thanked him and then reminded him about her medical bill. "What should I do, doctor Bala? How will I go about settling my medical expenses which I believe must be huge because you took care of me, you gave me my own room?"

"You gave her VIP treatment," Ronke said trying to lighten Lile's anxiety.

"I was actually coming to that," Doctor Bala grinned, "and now you have pre-empted me. But first thing first...."

He opened a drawer and brought out a small package and he pushed this to Lile on the office table. The man watched her closely as she opened it and stared blankly at the content, then looked at Dr Bala with some confusion.

Doctor Bala sighed softly with obvious disappointment.

"I see you don't have any idea how you came about this money?"

"Mine? The money is mine?" Lile looked amazed.

"Yes, it's all yours - five hundred and fifty dollars. But we took fifty dollars out of the money and bought some clothes and some personal items for you. So what you have there are five hundred dollars."

"But how – I really have no recollection about the money?" Lile stammered, still amazed.

"I was hoping you would tell me. We found the money in the pocket of your torn and blood-drenched jacket. We also found a shopping list with the money."

Dr Bala passed the list to Lile and again he carefully scrutinised her reaction as she read the list with Ronke. Again, Dr Bala looked disappointed. The list apparently provoked no memory.

"I'm sorry Dr Bala, don't recall either the money or this shopping list. And who is Ibrahim? Look, I wrote here- *'For Ibrahim's indulgence.'*

"Maybe he's my brother or my cousin or somebody I obviously know very well."

"Maybe he's your boyfriend," Ronke remarked and Lile blushed.

Doctor Bala watched Lile.

Lile looked at the doctor. "Actually the name sounds very familiar and soothing. I think Ibrahim might be my brother."

"He could even be your father," Doctor Bala said. "Anyway, I asked the nurses not to mention these things to you because I wanted to tell you myself."

Dr Bala paused and surveyed the two girls before continuing. "As for the medical bill, it would really be unfair for me to ask you to pay now that you can't afford to...."

"Please, you can have all these money, doctor Bala!" Lile cried. "Please you can have all of it and I know it won't be enough, but for starters, you can have everything until I locate my parents. I know they'll settle everything gratefully."

"I can ask my parents to help complete the remaining balance, Lile is like a sister, my mum adores her," Ronke looked at the old man, anxious on Lile's behalf but the old man waved all these aside.

"I want you to keep the money Lile, but remember you are still my patient and I'm only permitting you to go live with Ronke and her parents because I strongly believe a home environment would be strongly therapeutic for you psychologically, and will certainly speed up the process of recovery.

"Therefore, it will be very unfair for me to collect a single kobo from you until you are fully recovered and united with your family again.

"But all the same, I have here a medical expense bill for seventy-six thousand naira covering the basic cost of the operations and drugs as well as orthopaedic services. You can endorse it and keep a copy for your people when you finally meet with them.

The girls stared at him, speechless at his magnanimity.

"Now, I don't want you to feel any pressure whatsoever about this bill. The money can wait, even if it takes ten years to settle. You are getting fully recovered, that is in itself more than enough compensation for me."

Again that morning Lile felt overwhelmed with gratitude and tears gathered in her eyes. Without scanning the invoice, she picked up a pen from the table and endorsed the bill.

Doctor Bala handed a copy to Lile and smiled warmly at her.

Lile said, "I am grateful."

The doctor smiled. "I know."

After the girls finished thanking the old man and exchanging appreciation, the old doctor escorted them to the door.

Lile walked with the aid of two crutches that had been her constant companion for the past weeks and Ronke assisted her.

Doctor Bala stopped at the door, waved goodbye, and returned to his table to update Lile's medical file.

The sun was shining brightly and birds sang beautifully in the trees as Ronke Adams led Lile to the car park where the irrepressible Osage was waiting impatiently in his small car.

Osage rushed to them to help Lile as the two walked out of the building, followed by some nurses and one or two patients.

Carefully Lile was helped into the back seat and her crutches were handed over to her. Their luggage was already in the car booth. Ronke took the front seat and Osage drove off slowly with the nurses waving goodbye.

Lile waved goodbye to the nurses and as the gateman opened the gate and offered her a salute, something quite strange happened.

Suddenly a scene flashed through Lile's mind like a living, vivid picture.

It was a picture of a big mansion, flowers everywhere and a guard was opening a big, heavy black gate for her car to drive out and as the car passed, the gateman offered a smart salute with a friendly grin. For a second his eyes held her eyes and Lile shouted his name…

Osage and Ronke turned to stare at her, startled.

"Who is Sule?"

Lile stared at them in shock. "Our gateman, I saw him just now in my mind." Lile turned and gazed back at the receding hospital and the gateman still waving goodbye to her.

"I don't know how I know his name is Sule or that he is our gateman but I saw him clearly just now, and I also saw our house… a big house with flowers."

49

CHAPTER SIX

Doctor Dele Adams was the Head of Department of political science at the *Bayero* University, Kano. He totally belonged to the breed of radical and politically conscious academics whose vocal criticism of government had thoroughly irked the junta of the late Iron General, Sani Abacha. Besides, to compound Dr Adams sins in the eye of the former military dictator, Dr Adams had had the effrontery to fight Abacha from his own home state of Kano. And for this, Dr Dele Adams had paid a price.

Twice he had been abducted and locked up by the State Security Service for several months without end, denied access to all medical, social and legal rights. He lost his job in the university and his immediate family had been subjected to several bouts of primitive and crude intimidation. Even Ronke had been exposed to threats in her department of English in *Bayero* University as a final year student.

Then, just when all hope seemed to have been lost, when despair and helplessness stared the opposition in the face - then a divine miracle happened. The Iron General slumped to death in the company of imported Indian whores as it had was rumoured - a victim of his unholy excesses.

And the Nation heaved a sigh of relief, thinking tyranny would die with the Iron General.

And for a while, a certain calm did return to the traumatized country. Within the shortest time, Dr Adams and many of his vocal colleagues were released from detention and immediately reinstated to their former appointments and positions.

Many of these lecturers who had worn the appellation *"NADECO Lecturer"* as a mark of shame now wore the same toga as a token of pride, a status symbol of the struggle from unbridled despotism and their uncompromised stance and voices that refused to be cowed or silenced by the overwhelming rage of a ruthless and bullying tyrant.

* * * * * *

The Adams' home was a modest three-bedroom bungalow at the senior staff quarters of the rustic *Bayero* University. The house was one among several replicas surrounded in a hedge of hibiscus flowers and shrubs. The driveway was gravelled and led to a small garden in front of the building.

Like most academic homes, the house was well furnished but not vulgar. The furniture was of good quality but ageing. An electronic cabinet claimed the attention of the sitting room and other furniture had been arranged relative to this. A large wooden bookshelf bisected the sitting room from the dining area and an intimidating array of books crammed every available space of the shelf.

Also, besides Dr Adams favourite armchair rose a huge collection of magazines.

A computer aided painting of Kudirat Abiola took centre stage atop the bookshelf, which had so terrified the SSS on the day they came for Dr Adams. When they learnt the identity of the painter they quickly searched and confiscated all of Ronke's paintings, even the innocent ones, and all of these had been burnt before her eyes in a medieval show of torture.

And that night the double agony of the loss of her paintings and her father had sucked Ronke into a health crisis that nearly claimed her young life but for the timely arrival of doctor Bala in an ambulance.

"I had to wait until Abacha died before reproducing another painting of Kudi. She will always be my heroine," Ronke told Lile. "She will always be my inspiration...."

* * * * * *

Within a short time, Lile had become so adjusted to her new home that it was almost as though she had always been a member of the family. Mrs Adams offered her the use of the guestroom but Hugo had insisted that Lile would share Ronke's room. And Lile soon began to understand that whatever Hugo wanted in that home, Hugo always got.

Ronke had everything in her room. Her own TV set, video and CD player. A large, well-set cabinet bed occupied one corner of the room, close to the back window. Two vast wardrobes with a collection of boxes, luggage and clothes (dresses, T-shirts, slacks and native clothing.) Beside the bed, her make-up table and standing mirror. However, Ronke hated looking at the mirror.

"I know I'm beautiful and who cares what the mirror says?"

Next to the make-up set was another table and on top of this rested a beautiful 586 desktop PC complete with colour printer and *UPS*. It was clear to see that the Adams really loved and indulged their only child.

That first-day Ronke led Lile straight to her computer. "My parents got this for me as a graduation present some months ago. They say it'll keep me busy for the next one year before I begin my master's program."

Ronke had been exempted from the compulsory one-year National Service on health grounds.

"Would you like to see my computer paintings?" she asked Lile.

"Sure; I know they'll be beautiful."

The two girls took their chairs in front of the *PC* and Ronke booted up.

Ronke said, "I call them *computer paintings* because they are computer aided. I use the Corel Paintbrush environment but I can customise the easel to my own specifications. I have some of the paintings in printed hardcopy but I'd prefer you saw them first on the computer screen."

Ronke looked excited and Lile nods, infected by Ronke's enthusiasm for her artwork.

The first painting was titled *'GENESIS'*.

Everything about the painting was blue, different shades of blue, from a deep bluish-green backdrop to crystal blue circles and blue whorls of light. Submerged in the background, faint and immense, rose a faded blue, seven-layer pyramid. There was an overall wave-like quality to the painting like an image from a mirror submerged in a water-filled basin.

Lile kept staring at it, intrigued and curious yet completely at a loss as to the meaning of this painting. She could not help but recall Osage's teasing description of Ronke's paintings.

Lile turned to Ronke.

"I don't really comprehend this. Are you trying to depict creation the way it was at the very beginning?"

Ronke's face glowed with triumph. "I knew I could count on you to intuitively sense my paintings. Yes, Lile, I have tried to depict the entire universe the way I feel it may have been on that very instant when the Creator said *'Let there be light!'* And the pyramid represents the first seven days of creation just like the seven phases of life or colours of the rainbow."

Lile smiled at Ronke. "But then why the colour blue rather than a dazzling white?"

Ronke tried explaining, trying hard not to sound too technical. "There are three primal colours in creation - Blue, Red and Yellow. And for me blue represents life, red represents death or destruction and yellow is the unending transition between blue and red.

"On the other hand white is not a true colour. It has no dimension for me. It is rather an intangible quality, something that swings in the same realm and degree with qualities like time, like infinity and eternity. It is an intangible concept and will always remain so. True white is invisible, Lile, the colour of water."

Lile gaped open mouthed at her friend, never having suspected her of such esoteric depths.

Lile, "What?!"

Ronke laughed.

"Ronke you have thoroughly confused me."

Lile proffered her Elizabeth Arden wristwatch to Lile.

"Look at the face of my watch. This is what the world calls white. Like in white paper, white car, white chalk. I am not trying to deny the corporate existence of a white visual. You might as well try denying the existence of a black colour. But that is it, a simple visual of light, of motion, of time, a trick of the mind, an illusion imposed on our senses by our brain. And yet unreal."

Lile looked dazed. Ronke laughed, showing off her perfect gap-toothed charm.

"Even science agrees that what we call white is simply an illusion of the eyes and brain that is unable to separate colours packed together in motion. There are only three colours, Lile; Blue, Red and Yellow. All the rests are simply an illusion, simply a subjective scale of interpretation by our brain of these primal colours. We call them secondary colours. But for me, in the very beginning when the Creator said *let there be light!* He released only three colours - Blue, Yellow and Red. Everything began with blue and everything will end with red. That is why I chose blue for *Genesis.*"

'Bravo!' Lile clapped for her. 'Bravo professor very well said. You're really amazing, you know, really something else.'

The next painting was titled '*A LEGACY*'.

It was filled with different colours and what looked like a radiation of colours, different shapes, symbols and figures.

A central arc, more like a rainbow, spanned the painting from one edge of the easel to the other. The arc was made of two mirror sections of twelve distinct colours from black to a dazzling peak of white and back to black again. Each digit of colour was numbered from zero to twelve, the twelfth cube being a dazzling, radiant white. And from this radiant cube down to zero again.

Ronke said, "The arc traces Abiola's fulfilment from birth in poverty, to power and glory which climaxed on June 12th, to his death in detention, a poisoned victim of our democracy." There was a hint of pain in Ronke's voice.

"Abiola fulfilled his destiny, Lile. June 12 is his legacy."

"He was a good man", Lile said softly. "I read a lot about him in the hospital."

Ronke corrected. "My father loved that man like he was a tin god. He was a decent man. And nobody will ever take that away from him."

There were nine other paintings. Most of them traced subtle political undertones and some of them explored the meaning of life and death. Some of the paintings were fascinating and still some them were superfluous, had no rhythm or reason behind them, despite Ronke's forced rationalisation and articulation. But at the end of it all, the girl's audacity and arrogance fascinated Lile. Her talent was also a bit scary.

Ronke switched off the computer and turned to Lile for an appraisal.

"What do you think about my work?"

Lile hesitated.

Ronke smiled. "Be honest, I can take it."

"I think you have bottled up a lot of anguish and frustration inside you and these paintings are mostly an outlet, a vent for your despair."

Ronke stared at Lile, surprised. She had not expected that from Lile. Most people generally thought that Ronke was crazy or pretending to a western level of sophistication and obscurism.

Lile said, "look at your paintings again Ronke - none has love, family or happiness as a central theme."

Ronke got out of her chair, flopped down on the bed, and hugged Hugo to her chest.

"Hugo has never known true happiness, Lile. He's just a morphine freak, living in the world of Morpheus."

"Don't be silly. You are the liveliest person I know. And look around you; everything speaks of harmony and beauty. Everything glows with love."

"People say life is beautiful because they are filled with hope and expectations. How can life be beautiful for Hugo who has never known hope? He is twenty-two now but many people believe he will not live to know twenty-five". Ronke hugged and caressed her teddy. "Poor Hugo, how can you possibly make paintings about love and happiness?"

Lile came to the bed and embraced Hugo and his desolate friend.

"It's not fair to people who love you, Ronke, it's not fair."

Lile looked upset and did not know what else to say and tears started running down her face. "Life is beautiful, it will always be beautiful."

* * * * * *

That night Lile experienced another nightmare. She dreamt she was trapped in a burning car, screaming and struggling futilely to free herself. She woke up screaming and bathed in sweat. Ronke stood over her, still shaking her and looking worried and scared.

"Oh my God, I was trapped in a burning car!"

"It was only a dream, Lile," Ronke said lamely. "Here," and she pushed Hugo to Lile. "You can sleep with Hugo on your side of the bed."

Holding hands both girls prayed and then turned off the light. They talked deep into the night before sleep finally came.

CHAPTER SEVEN

I brahim Dambaba had finally capitulated to the protracted and relentless attrition of his close family's primitive blackmail.

Besides, Lile's death - he had come to accept the inevitable term - her loss had broken his fighting spirit and his sense of defiance. For him, life had become a rather drab and monotonous routine. Lile Yusuf had disappeared from Ibrahim's life with all the spontaneous warmth and enthusiasm with which she had filled his existence.

Ibrahim negotiated his car expertly between the unpredictable Lagos traffic. He was on his way to keep a reluctant appointment in Festac town with cruel destiny.

The afternoon weather looked brisk and mild after the late morning rain shower and the Lagos crowd was slowly emerging from their shelter to continue their hustling.

Some things would always be the same in Lagos, Ibrahim mused to himself. Everybody seemed so busy, dashing here and there in search of the perfect deal and business tradeoffs.

Ten weeks … ten weeks since Lile Yusuf disappeared without a trace. And in a city as big and populated as Lagos, who could possibly trace one missing girl? Conservatively, ten people were reported or declared missing on a daily basis in Lagos. It was a *no-man's-land* and some things would never change.

Nevertheless, for the daughter of a high profile personality like Major General M.S Yusuf to vanish in this town and nobody seemed to care or bother really spoke volumes as to the level of decadence and cold-bloodedness of this depraved city.

Even the General himself seemed to have finally lost hope and caved into the inevitable loss of his only daughter. He had been out of the country for the past one week after an unprecedented eight weeks stay in Lagos while organising the search for Lile. Finally, last week, the General turned tail and fled the country to nurse his broken heart.

Ibrahim sighed as he swerved into Festac road. He pulled sharply into a side street and began to slow down as his destination approached. J-close, Road 23, Festac town. Ambassador Yahaya Buhari's home.

Ibrahim sighed again, like a drowning man approaching his new destiny. Dreading the inexorable.

* * * * *

Halima Buhari was not yet sixteen years old. She still had that shy, baby innocence about her.

Voluptuous, fair complexioned and reserved, she had only recently graduated from Command Secondary School, Jos and was anxiously awaiting her *SSCE* result.

Two weeks ago that result had been the most important event of her young life until her father called her into his study and succinctly told her she had only one month within which to prepare herself emotionally and psychologically for marriage.

Halima kept staring at her father, with dread and the mixed feeling of fascination and disbelief.

The Ambassador continued. "You know Ibrahim Dambaba? he has kindly asked for your hand in marriage and our family has agreed that he is the right match for you."

For some strange reason, the old man would not look Halima in the face. He kept fiddling and fussing with some papers on his desk as he delivered his message.

Now he looked up at her.

"Do you have any question, Halima?"

"No Baba," she answered automatically but she had a thousand and one questions.

Halima Buhari knew Ibrahim Dambaba very well. They were close family associates and Ibrahim was a close pal of her uncle Kabiru.   Halima also knew Ibrahim Dambaba to be betrothed to Lile Yusuf, the General's only daughter and heir.

Besides, Major General M.S Yusuf was her father's friend and business partner. So the three families were strongly intertwined in several overt and subtle ways.

Now in her inner mind, Halima Buhari wondered why in this world would her father even consider jeopardising successful and long-standing friendship with General M.S Yusuf.

Halima was finally released from her father's presence and quickly ran in search of her mother. She found Hajia in the garden behind the main house, obviously waiting for her. Two of her older, married sisters were also waiting with her mum.

"Mama, I don't want to marry Ibrahim Dambaba," Halima blurted out as soon as she saw her mother.

The women quickly calmed down her fears. It was from her mother that Halima would learn for the first time about Lile's tragedy. Halima had been in boarding school then and had heard nothing about this.

Slowly and professionally the Buhari women folk built up a powerful and magnetic image of her husband-to-be in Halima's mind and his commendable qualities. In the end, even Halima herself found it quite hard containing her excitement and good fortune for landing such a handsome and eligible bachelor like Ibrahim Dambaba.

"What if she's not dead, mama, then what will I do? What if he still prefers her to me when she returns?"

"Oh the poor girl is dead, Halima," her mother smiled at Halima to ease her fears. "You know these Lagos people. She was probably the victim of some ritual killers.

"Even if by chance she's still alive," one of Halima's sisters added, "Lile Yusuf can find herself another pilot. Ibrahim Dambaba is not the only man in Lagos, you know."

* * * * * *

One evening Halima and her friend Hanatu were alone in the garden and discussing the coming event when one of the servants ushered in Ibrahim Dambaba. The two girls burst into embarrassed laughter.

Halima introduced her friend shyly and Ibrahim talked and teased both girls until Hajia came and joined them. Hajia Buhari exchanged pleasantries with Ibrahim.

"Is the General back yet from London? We are hoping he makes the *fatiha* so people can stop gossiping and speculating. I want people to be shamed for all their nasty gossiping." Hajia sounded quite testy.

"My father spoke with him on the phone yesterday. He said he will be around for the wedding although he's still mourning his daughter."

"He is a good man, and may Allah grant eternal rest to Lile Yusuf."

Hajia allowed herself some few minutes of silent contemplation of Ibrahim while the two girls avoided Ibrahim Dambaba's eyes.

"What about you, Ibrahim?" Hajia said finally. "How do you really feel about all these? You have hardly said anything personal about all of these since the agreement was struck for you to marry Halima."

Ibrahim tried laughing. "What can I say, Hajia? I am grateful to Allah for finding for me a wife as young and beautiful as Halima."

He tried to grab Halima's hands but she covered her face, shy and embarrassed while the others laughed at her.

After this, the conversation turned to other mundane and impersonal topics and Ibrahim Dambaba silently heaved a sigh of relief.

She was such a shy, young gazelle, Halima, he thought, but what choice did both of them have? Their families had chosen both of them for each other and that was all there was to it. After all, the family had also chosen Lile Yusuf for him back then and everything worked out fine for both of them.

Looking at Halima, Ibrahim felt some pity for her but then dynasties are established by systematic positioning and ruthless calculations.

CHAPTER EIGHT

D ear Diary,

My whole world is filled with deja vu. I am entering the twelfth week of my stay in Limbo. The land of Amnesia is not a gracious host to a victim of deja vu.

Dr Bala says relax. I should take things the way they come. I should not give way to latent hysteria. This dark and spooky feeling of claustrophobia. But Dr Bala is only hiding his anxiety. I overheard him confessing yesterday to Dr Adams when we took Ronke to the hospital for her routine checkup. He said what I really needed was a shock from my past. Maybe an encounter with someone or some people who I know very well.

Dear Diary, what would I have done without Ronke and her family? They are so nice and caring. Dr Adams will sit us down for hours and lecture us on his favourite topic: politics. Yesterday he said that the selection and emergence of Obasanjo as a presidential candidate was a calculated attempt by the Minna mafia to impose anarchy on the country. The word "Minna Mafia" has a very familiar ring to it for me. I don't know why.

Osage is my friend. He probably understands that I cannot date him or share any meaningful relationship with him. He has such a generous, warm personality that it is almost hard to resist him sometimes. To help my resolve, Ronke showed me the pictures of all his women. Osage is an irresponsible playboy but still, I like him as a friend.

Osage has driven me all over Kano as he promised he would but yet we have not run into anybody who has even remotely shown any interest in me. Besides, I have this strange feeling deep inside me that I have never lived in Kano before. But then Diary, if this is the case, how come I speak very fluent Hausa? I also speak Yoruba fluently but that is not so surprising to me. I believe, and Ronke does too, that I am a Lagos girl. Dr Adams is even planning for a two weeks trip for Ronke and me to go to Lagos and stay with Ronke's Aunt, Bola.

Perhaps the sound and visuals of Lagos will break me out from the land of Limbo. It is a very exciting thought. Everything I hear or read about Lagos seems familiar. Dear Diary, I am an Omo Eko!

About Ronke. Ronke's illness upsets me. Why should one little human being suffer so much? She looks so cheerful and brave outwardly but she keeps thinking about death. Each time I run into the bathroom and find her shivering and vomiting, I feel dreadful and helpless inside my spirit. Dr Bala wants her flown abroad but I don't think her parents have that kind of money. They have taken her to different kind of churches for prayer and miracle but it never really works out for Ronke. She even jokes about it. She says that she has too much unbelief for miracles to work for her. I see her parents suffering much more than their

68

daughter and it seems so unfair that such a nice family are victims to such a monstrous destiny. Hugo calls it karma. A mission karma. And personally, I think that Hugo reads too much esoteric literature for his own good. But why should someone take on such a dreadful mission to make people suffer? Mrs Adams says if they were less literate, they would long since have labelled Ronke an Abiku child.

Ronke is a member of the Sickle Cell Society. The society believes there is no universal cure available for sickle cell sufferers. During a sickle cell crisis, the red blood cells change shape after oxygen has been released and agglutinate, causing blockage of the tiny red blood vessels. The pain and agony can be excruciating and horrendous, alleviated only by the administration of strong painkillers like pethadine and morphine, it is such a dreadful ordeal.

Over time, patients experience damage to organs such as their liver, kidney, lungs, heart and spleen. Current research of the disorder has resulted in the use of Bone Marrow transplant as a possible cure, and further treatment called hydroxyurea which significantly reduces the number of painful crisis is currently undergoing trials. I pray every night for a cure. For Ronke's sake, for her parents' sake, and for Hugo's sake.

Dear Diary, help me to pray to Allah, the Merciful, the Compassionate, the Beneficent. Pray to Allah to give all of us in this family the courage to understand our plight and pain. May Allah forgive our sins.

* * * * * *

The three young people chose an outdoor fast food joint off Ibrahim-Taiwo road. It was a cool Sunday evening and the weather was mild and slightly breezy. The cafe was largely patronised by young people and their laughter and happiness filled the air.

There was something buoyant about Kano these days ever since the death of the Iron General. Prior to his death, Kano was an iron state, the home of Power Brokers who arrogated to themselves ultimate control over the lives of the common folks of Kano.

However, overnight all that had changed. The very air that evening was fresh with the sense of liberty blowing across the country:

"When the news came to us in prison that Abacha was dead," Dr Adams had told Lile, "it was unbelievable the happiness and joy that united everybody in that prison that day. We were all laughing and shaking hands, all of us, both wardens, prisoners and detainees. The whole country and even condemned armed robbers were shouting and shaking hands in congratulations because a man had lost his life… may this country never witness such a shocking spectacle again."

70

Osage had taken the two girls out that evening as a treat for Ronke who was recuperating from her last ordeal in the hands of Sickle cell anaemia.

Ronke's face was a bit swollen and there were painful blisters on her lips which made her wince each time she laughed or smiled. Like Lile, she was simply dressed in a white, flower print gown.

Both girls had gone shopping when Lile came to stay and vainly tried dressing alike for effects.

Today Lile was laughing uninhibitedly at Ronke and Osage, fencing with words in their perpetual mock battles with witty repartee.

Lile had all but recovered physically except for the plaster-cast still on her leg, which Dr Bala had promised to remove next month; but meanwhile, she was still consigned to her crutches. Her face shone with mirth and her golden eyes twinkled with pleasure. Her hair had all but grown luxuriously and heads kept turning admiringly in her direction. Lile Yusuf was truly a beautiful young woman in her prime...

Ronke threatened Osage for the 100th time. "If by tomorrow you don't return my lighthouse family CDs, then just be careful because I'll poison you the first opportunity I get." Ronke tried to keep a straight face. "Don't think I am joking, Osage! I am a woman provoked beyond my ability for compassion."

Osage chuckled. "I know you're deadly serious Ronke. I really, really promise that you will have your CDs tomorrow. But if you must poison me, then let it come like in poisoned apples!"

They girl laughed at Osage.

"I really, really love poisoned apples, you know," Osage teased. "Especially the fine Indian variety. Luscious virgin Indian apples!" Osage smacked his lips and kissed the air. "Way to go, men!"

Their drinks and snacks finally came and Osage raised his glass and proposed a toast.

"To the two most exciting girls in the world. Ebony and Ivory, I call them. May your days always be exciting and adventurous. To Lile, I say, you have a history. And to Ronke, I say, you have a future. May your days be filled with laughter and happiness."

They clinked glasses together and drank. The girls wiped their mouth off fruit juice and Osage dropped his empty glass of beer and refilled same again.

He turned to Lile.

"I heard both of you are planning to spend the Christmas season in Lagos. Is that wise?"

"What's wrong with Lagos?" Ronke demanded. "I've spent much of my life in Kano and I think I'm due for a change of scenery. Besides, Lile has seen enough of Kano, she strongly feels her family are probably somewhere in Lagos, or Abuja."

"But you saw how Lagos erupted last July when Abiola died? The town was torn apart. People were looting and rampaging, destroying home and lives. The Christmas season will provide those crazy Lagos hoodlums with another opportunity for mayhem.

"If that doesn't work, I can almost guarantee you that this crippling fuel scarcity is sure to trigger off another bout of madness in Lagos. Sincerely Lile, if you ask me, I really don't feel that Lagos is the place to be around during the Christmas period."

Lile sipped her juice and looked at Osage anxiously. She could not remember what had happened in Lagos or any other part of the country with Abiola's death. She only knew that Abiola's death had shocked and saddened many people unlike the extreme reaction of unbridled joy that Abacha's death had provoked. Lile turned to Ronke for assurance.

"Don't mind Osage, Lile. Don't let him scare you off. He only wants us to stay in Kano so he can keep trying to win you over and break your defences."

Lile laughed. "Is that your plan, Osage?"

Osage shook his head. "How can that be my plan? See, I am just concerned about your welfare, baby. Moreover, I believe your family is somewhere here in Kano. If you don't believe me then look at yourself in the mirror. Mummy believes that you are a Fulani girl and so do I. And now tell me how many Fulani families you'll find in Lagos?"

"I may look Fulani, but I could actually be a Yoruba girl or even an Ibo girl. Some Ibo girls look like me, in fact, they are as beautiful as sylphs...."

Osage sniffed at that. "I'll bet my last kobo you're no *okoro* girl, besides you don't speak one word of Ibo."

Again they found themselves arguing and laughing, trying to place Lile's tribe. Osage made the wildest conjectures. He said the name Lile was the short form of the Fulani name: *Osage aieeeooo Au's Wayahila ula lile aishatue!* And it meant: Osage, please I desperately love you with all my life, marry me, my knight!

Their laughter receded into the darkening October sky.

CHAPTER NINE

The time was way past eight o'clock on the wall clock that Sunday evening when it finally happened.

The shock for Lile was total. It was clothed in such a crude and tragic force as to leave the girl utterly shattered and gasping for breath.

Mrs Adams was preparing a late dinner in the kitchen and the two girls were assisting her, still glowing from their exciting outing with the irrepressible Osage. They were discussing and laughing while Dr Adams waited impatiently in the parlour for his dinner, watching television and looking clearly bored.

At last Mrs Adams packed her husband's dinner on a tray with his mandatory after dinner bottle of beer and Lile carried these to the parlour, still laughing at something Ronke had said about her father's appetite.

Mrs Adams and Ronke were getting ready to move to the dining room when from the parlour came the unmistakable sound of crashing cutleries and breaking ceramics and glass.

"Oh my goodness," Mrs Adams gasped, "Lile has tripped!"

Lile stood in the parlour, rooted to the floor, and all around her broken glass and plates and the sorry sight of Dr Adams ruined dinner.

Lile stood frozen solid and starring with an unbelieving and hypnotic horror at the beaming face of Ibrahim Dambaba and his young bride, surrounded by their friends and families.

Lile Yusuf was completely horrified and mesmerised and tears spilt down her cheeks.

Ronke and Mrs Adams rushed out from the kitchen and stopped short at the unnatural sight of Lile, frozen like a statue; and from Lile to the TV and from the TV back to Lile, and all the while Dr Adams was shaking Lile in his panic, demanding from her what was wrong....

"Ibrahim," Lile said softly. "My fiancé, Ibrahim Dambaba... he is marrying another woman."

Lile covered her face and began to cry and Mrs Adams held the trembling girl to herself.

"Poor child, oh you poor child."

Ronke stared at the radiant face of Ibrahim and his bride on the TV screen with some fascination. And to herself, "Bastard, you couldn't even wait three months for her..."

* * * * * *

Things would never be the same again for Lile Yusuf as she looked out of the car window at the rushing scenery of Kano metropolis as their car sped to the airport. It was ten o'clock, Monday morning and the General's plane would touch down on Kano soil by 11:30 am. He was coming on a chartered flight.

The morning weather looked downcast, as though it would rain later in the day, and Lile felt how appropriate the weather reflected her mood. Depression...?

Yesterday night Dr Bala had rushed triumphantly to the house to sedate Lile Yusuf after the shocking trauma of recognising Ibrahim Dambaba and his bride, little Halima Buhari.

Lile's memory was returning in phases, still in bits and pieces but the doctor asked her to relax. What mattered most was that she had bridged a major blockade and every memory digit would begin to fall in place on their own.

Doctor Bala said, "It is natural if you feel very depressed for the next few weeks, considering what has happened. Nevertheless, remember your life must never be the same again. You have been granted a rare opportunity to start life afresh."

He was a wonderful man, that doctor, risking his life to run to Lile's aid that Sunday night.

The Adams family were escorting Lile to the airport to meet her father and Dr Adams had absented himself from his classes to drive them to the airport. They were all silent in the Mercedes, even Hugo. Suddenly things were not the same anymore, and Lile's imminent exit from their lives left everybody downcast.

Nobody dared be the first to raise the issue. They were all lost in their own thoughts and depression.

Dr Adams had gotten in touch with the General yesterday night, for Lile had recollected seven different phone numbers with which to reach her father.

Dr Adams had finally gotten through to the General on his cellular number around midnight, while Lile slept, sedated from Dr Bala's prescribed drugs. It took quite some time to convincing M.S Yusuf that the call was not a cruel hoax designed to torment a bereaved father.

Dr Adams had even been forced to minutely describe the girl to her father. Her dimples, the colour of her eyes and her physical stature. Doctor Adams really felt embarrassed listening to the old man crying on the telephone. The General kept on expressing his gratitude and evoking all the blessings of Allah on Dr Adams, clearly reluctant to drop the phone.

Ronke broke the silence in the car. "Hugo will go with you to Lagos, Lile."

Her parents turned to glare at her with consternation but Lile pulled the girl to herself. "You are the only sister I have, Ronke."

Mrs Adams said, "Even if you are going to Lagos with your sister, it's not going to be permanent I hope?"

Ronke smiled. "Hugo will never run away from home, mummy. We only want to help Lile acclimatise to that strange barbaric city, Lagos."

* * * * * *

At the airport, Lile was filled again with a strong sense of de ja vu. "I've been here before," She told them.

At the airport, they waited anxiously in the visitors' lounge for the General. His plane did not come until past 1:00 pm and by then the family were urgently scrutinising every likely man and eyeing Lile questioningly.

Lile herself was stressed up, uncertain whether she would recognise her own father. She leaned restlessly on her crutches, eyes darting here and there. Ronke kept telling her, "Don't dare disappoint me, girl. Blood must always prove to be thicker than water."

But Father and daughter recognised each other instantly. The General was dark and tall, in flowing white caftan, cell phone and briefcase in both hands; and the briefcase slipped out of his hand, as father and child moved towards each other and arms wound around one another in an unbreakable embrace.

They were crying and laughing, a tragic spectacle in that crowded Kano International Airport.

Later Lile introduced her father to her new family. The General shook hands all round and pumped Doctor Adams' hands gratefully. He held Mrs Adams' hands and she could see tears gathering in his eyes.

"Madam," the General said in his deep, sonorous baritone. "I am a proud and arrogant man and I have everything a man can dream of, money, power and influence, but all has been worthless to me without my daughter.

"Madam, through you people, and through the goodness of that medical Doctor, Allah has again humbled and enriched my life beyond measure by returning Lile to me. We had giving her up for dead."

Again the old man shook hands all around and held Lile tightly. "Only Allah understands how to teach a man the valuable lesson of understanding his priorities better."

Lile let go of her crutches and leaned fully on her father, smiling confidently. "From now on I have no need for crutches," and limping slowly, she led the way to the car pack.

Ronke picked up the discarded crutches in dismay and carried it for Lile all the way to the car pack. Even Lile herself might not fully suspect how much she craved the General's approval for her show of courage and determination, for children would eternally measure themselves relative to their parents.

CHAPTER TEN

T
he time was about four o'clock in the evening when the General drove into the premises of the Intensive Care Hospital with Lile and Ronke. Doctor Adams had graciously surrendered his car for their use.

At the hospital, news had quickly spread and the staff came out in a crowd to welcome Lile's father.

The General shook hands with every one of them; nurses, doctors, interns and non-medical staff of the hospital. M.S Yusuf was filled with so much gratitude to these people who had plucked his only child from the very jaws of death.

Doctor Bala led the General and the two girls to his office. One of the nurses came in with soft drinks and served the guests.

Dr Bala winked at Lile and his eyes twinkled with mischief.

"I told you all would work out well".

Lile smiled shyly. "I am eternally grateful, sir."

The General said, "I have been informed about the incredible things you have done for Lile. How you plucked her from the jaws of certain death. Her several operations, how you fed her, how you sheltered her without even knowing who she was...

"Doctor, I want to say with all sincerity that we owe you a debt that can never be fully repaid. May Allah bless you forever and may your name be written in the holy book of paradise."

The doctor was moved. "I wish we were able to do more for Lile. She has only partially recovered her memory due to the shocking marriage of her fiancé she saw on the news.

Lile clearly needs advanced psychotherapy, which I am unable to provide for her. She needs a specialist to accelerate the healing process. But physically I can assure you that she's as fit as a fiddle."

"I'll be leaving for London in two weeks' time. Lile will be coming with me. Ronke will also be coming with us. Lile told me that you had advised her parents to fly her out for advanced therapy?"

"She needs exposure to better medical facilities and professional care in the field of anaemia." Dr Bala looked at Ronke and then at the General and at Lile. "God is wonderful."

Doctor Bala did not say more but was thinking how the little seed of kindness the Adams family had sown in offering their home to a lonely, lost child was multiplying and blessing their lives to the extent of affording positive hope for their own sickle cell anaemic child, Ronke Adams.

The General was still speaking. "I will be needing the files of their medical history, especially that of Ronke."

"You'll have them. Lile's file is a bit scanty for the brief nature of her situation and stay with us but we have done our best. As for the leg cast, we were thinking of removing the POP next month. She suffered multiple fractures but that can be easily done in Lagos or in London."

"One last detail, doctor." The General said and smiled at Lile. "She gave me a medical bill from you for her treatment. Seventy-six thousand naira."

Dr Bala laughed and waved that aside good-naturedly. "Oh, that was part of her therapy. If I had just let her go like that, she would have kept worrying and feeling guilty.

"But with that bill, I hoped to help her relax and free her mind from any sense of obligation or tension. It is a simple medical psychology. She actually owes the hospital nothing."

"Doctor Adams told me the same thing. He said you had discussed it with his wife. However, Dr Bala, I do not intend to insult your charity. Still, I want you to keep doing for other helpless accident victims what you have done for Lile,"

The general opened his briefcase and handed a signed check to doctor Bala.

"It's a check for fifteen million naira, doctor Bala, we present to you this draft with the strongest sense of humility and gratitude. May Allah shower his blessings on you and your hospital employees."

The doctor held the check with a slightly trembling hand and slowly he removed thick spectacles from his eyes and stared near sighted at his guests, shaken and thoroughly speechless. Fifteen million naira!

* * * * * *

Osage said with some feeling, "General, you have Lile's eyes. She has eyes the colour of fresh honey. And maybe that's why she's special."

Lile and Ronke had come to say goodbye to Osage and the General had driven them to his two-bedroom apartment in the heart of the *Sabon-Gari.*

Osage had been surprised to see them but like Ronke told him, a world of events had exploded within the space of a couple of hours.

"Osage thinks he's in love with Lile," Ronke said impishly and Osage stuttered and stammered, embarrassed and flustered but M.S. Yusuf laughed and placed a hand on Osage's shoulder.

"It's nothing to be ashamed of, son. If I were your age, I would also be in love with a girl like Lile. She really is a beautiful girl."

Osage found it easy to agree with this sentiment. "She's something else, sir".

They stood by the Mercedes in front of Osage's apartment. Some little kids and their dogs played nearby, laughing and alive. And in the distance, the sun was setting slowly beyond the house roofs.

Lile smiled, a hint of tears in her voice.

"I came to say goodbye, Osage. We are leaving for Lagos first thing in the morning tomorrow. Ronke and I.

"I can never forget you, Osage." Lile's voice broke and tears coursed down her face. "You are my friend. You and Ronke will always be my brother and sister."

For once Osage was completely at a loss for words himself and feelings choked him. He proffered his hands to Lile and they shook hands solemnly.

"Goodbye Lile. We will see again."

"We will... I know we will, Osage."

He held Lile's crutches as she got into the vehicle. The others bade him goodbye and Ronke promised to bring back delicacies from Lagos for him.

"Besides, you can keep the lighthouse CDs since you love them so much."

Osage waved goodbye and as the car began to move he ran to Lile's side. "Lile, there is hope beyond every rainstorm. No matter how dark the cloud seems to be, sunlight will always break through each morning. Always remember this, baby."

Lile promised never to forget and Osage kept waving goodbye until the car turned a bend and disappeared out of sight. He let down his hands and stood for a while lost and uncertain, staring vacantly at the playing kids and barking dogs in the street.

Osage turned and walked back to his house. The world was filled with pretty girls but a princess would always be a princess and no man would ever cross her paths without being richer for his experience and good fortune.

Osage paused briefly at his door, raised his hand in salute to the lingering memory of her presence, and then shut the door.

CHAPTER ELEVEN

The ride from the Lagos International Airport to Dolphin Heights Estate would ever remain an indescribable experience for Lile.

The General's chauffeur, Musa, had come with the jeep to pick them up and with him was…

"Maureen!" Lile gasped in surprise. She turned to Ronke still amazed. "It's my roommate, Maureen. She's my friend!"

The two roommates embraced one another and Lile formally introduced the two girls.

In the car, the General explained that he had asked Musa to pick Maureen up from school on his way to the airport. "I am happy you recognised her at once. It's a good sign, your amnesia will recede soon."

Lile chortled. "It's good to see you again Maureen. How's LASU, our course mates and friends?"

"Everybody is worried about you, Lile. You have missed a Semester in school."

"That means Lile has an extra year?" Ronke asked.

"Yes, but only an extra second semester. We are on our final semester before she vanished."

Lile had so many questions she wanted to ask but the General cautioned her to take things easy. Maureen was not running away.

The long ride to Dolphin Heights was memorable to Lile Yusuf in so many ways. She was filled with deja vu and the power of foreknowledge. The route, the people and buildings exerted subtle and compelling challenges to memory, prodding her sense of recollection and Lile kept describing impressions to Ronke who had never been to Lagos before.

"I can never be a stranger in Lagos," Lile Laughed.

From the front, watching his daughter casually, M.S Yusuf felt inwardly buoyant and happy. The healing process had begun for Lile and like Doctor Bala had advised, the unexpected appearance of her roommate and friend Maureen had gone a long way in dispelling the persistent veil of amnesia. Allah is merciful the old man said to himself.

* * * * * *

No. 3 Allen close, Dolphin Heights Estate. The white marble mansion towered high into the sky, resplendent and awesome behind the massive, black gates.

The gateman opened the gates for the jeep and as the powerful car passed through the gateman raised his hands briefly in a smart salute.

And Lile smiled, with tears of gratitude.

Ronke said, "I guess that is Sule."

"That is Sule."

Ronke stared around. For Ronke, the surrounding beauty and opulence around them left her breathless. The beauty of Dolphin Heights painted a sharp contrast with some of the slums of Lagos and while their car had cruised the 3rd Mainland Bridge, reputed to be the longest bridge in Africa, Ronke had stared with shamed disbelieve at the what was probably the worst ghetto in the world, a slum of fishermen huts floating in brackish water, it stretched for miles and miles and she saw canoes crisscrossing the water-city.

"Oh my God," Ronke had cried out in amazement. "They live on water!"

"They are Ijaw fishermen and their family," Maureen told her.

Lile said, "They are the face of Lagos on international TV."

"They and Molue buses!"

The girls laughed but M.S Yusuf said nothing. He brought out his mobile and began dialling a number.

Ronke said, "Hugo is so speechless, so much and yet so little."

She felt as though they had passed through decaying, decrepit ghettoes to get to this oceanic island haven of the rich and powerful. Two extreme worlds juxtaposed in time and space.

Lile's home was a palace in every sense of the word. The house seemed enclosed in exotic flowers and fruit trees, well-trimmed garden and hedges, green and vibrant.

Royal palms spaced the gravelled drive in double columns like sentinels.

Ronke turned to gape at Lile and her father. "This place looks like a Caribbean hotel… It is like those beautiful and magical scenes from Arabian Nights… Lile, how can you forget a place like this!"

Even Lile was looking around, dazzled and amazed. She had held a vague impression of the place in her mind but certainly nothing as frightening and grandiloquent as this!

The jeep purred to a halt in front of the foyer, a waiting orderly opened the door for M.S. Yusuf, and the General turned to his daughter. "Welcome home, Lile."

* * * * * *

For two days Lile Yusuf was closed in the past, rediscovering her history and roots. The house helps were all eager to serve her and the two girls were waited on hands and foot and feted like princesses.

The process of self-discovery was both a thrilling and painful pilgrimage for Lile Yusuf. Painful for the simple reason that her history and happiness had obviously been built around Ibrahim Dambaba.

He was everywhere, Ibrahim Dambaba. His laughing face mocked her from her collection of pictures. His voice echoed from all her letters and from a hundred notes and scraps which she had carefully treasured in a vanity chest. Lile Yusuf's room was haunted with the overbearing presence of Ibrahim. She recalled posters, clothes, jewellery and several personal stuffs as gifts she had once received from Ibrahim. And each little memory evoked such anguish, like the agony of an asthmatic victim, asphyxiating for lack of air, desperately struggling for oxygen.

Lile Yusuf suffered in silence, hiding her pain even from the prying eyes of Hugo.

Lile's room faced the back of the estate and from her balcony, she looked right into the shimmering swimming pool and, beyond the pool and wall, the ever inscrutable, surging ocean...

On several occasions, the two girls would sit here and ponder the world and Ronke's mind would thrill to the exhilarating defiance posed by the pulsating orchestration of elemental symphony, frames and frames of eternal harmony and chaos as Ronke phrased it....

* * * ** *

For that first week, visitors kept pouring into M.S Yusuf's home, to rejoice and felicitate with him for the joyful reunion with his daughter. Because of this influx of guests their home buzzed from morning to night with relatives, friends; the General's military colleagues and his several business associates, well-wishers who had all come to show their sense of solidarity and neighbourliness.

Time without number, Lile Yusuf and Ronke Adams were compelled to recount the amazing story of Lile's forced sojourn in Kano, a helpless young girl with no roots, no history, no memory. It was such a scary scenario, and the visitors shuddered and wondered at such vagaries of kismet. And to the last man, they all blessed the courage and goodness of doctor Bala, for how many doctors in the country now would be found willing to risk reputation, money and resources to treat a dying, accident victim?

Indeed, they all agreed that fifteen million naira was not enough compensation for such a selfless and charitable service.

Among the very early visitors was Lile's Aunt, Hajia Hauwawu Abdulkadir Abubakar, the General's stepsister. She flew in from Abuja to see the miracle with her "own eyes."

Lile and her aunt were inseparably fond of each other and to a large extent, her aunt had played the role of surrogate mother to Lile until her marriage to multi-billionaire businessman, Alhaji Halilu Abdulkadir Abubakar, a couple of years back.

Often, Lile spent her vacations in Abuja at their home, especially during some of the General's prolonged business trips outside the country.

It was from her Aunt that Lile was finally able to clear the puzzle as to the source of the dollars found with her in Kano.

Hajia Hauwawu said the money must have been part of one thousand dollars she had given Lile as a birthday gift two days before her ill-fated flight to Kano. "Ten pieces of one hundred dollar notes, all ten of them, brand new mints."

The two girls confirmed this. "Except for the fifty dollars spent by doctor Bala to buy some clothes and stuffs for me, they are all in brand new one hundred dollar bills. Maybe I lost the rest at the site of the accident.

"I was rushed to the hospital without any luggage."

Hajia Hauwawu held her niece close to herself, loving and tender. "Allah be praised for your life, Lile Yusuf. That is all that matters to me. And when you come back from London, you will come and live for some time with us in Abuja". Hajia turned to Ronke, "And you too, Ronke".

"And Hugo". Lile smiled.

"And Hugo, too!" Hajia Hauwawu brushed treacherous tears from her eyes. "Oh you really gave us the shock of our lives, Lile. The great M. S. Yusuf was reduced to a ghost of himself within the first one month. Now he will be a more serious father, more available than before. Allah be praised and glorified, forever."

CHAPTER TWELVE

He stood by the swimming pool, in front of her empty balcony, gazing up at the drawn window blind, eyes filled with surprise and despair. Thus he had waited for several hours, Ibrahim Dambaba, in silence now because of the futility of calling her name and pleading for an audience.

Lile Yusuf would not see him, would not talk to him, would not have anything to do with him ever again. He had been banished from her life like a bad memory.

Just like that…

Ibrahim Dambaba turned and paced restlessly around the pool and again paused to stare at the drawn blind, running fingers through his hair in frustration.

He had been trying to make contact with Lile for the best part of one week and each time she would lock herself in her room and drown out his pleading voice with her CD player. Only once did she send Ronke Adams to tell him to leave her alone.

"Leave her alone", Ronke Adams' eyes burnt with contempt and Ibrahim pleaded and cried, all to no avail.

"Leave Lile Yusuf alone Ibrahim, her life has been shattered and broken, please just let her be; besides don't you owe a certain amount of responsibility to your new wife to stay away from Lile Yusuf?"

"No, you don't really understand!" Ibrahim tried explaining but the door was slammed shut in his face.

And still, he kept trying. Lile would not return his phone calls, all his letters were returned unread and all their mutual friends were equally denied access to Lile Yusuf.

Only the General seemed to understand but even he confessed his unpreparedness to interfere in his daughter's decision.

M. S. Yusuf said, "Ibrahim, give her time. It is nobody's fault, but Lile is still hurting. And you know that for now, she is still not a hundred percent upstairs? Maybe given time she will again recall memories that will soften her attitude to you. Give her time, Ibrahim…"

Not Ibrahim. He was practically living at Allen close. He stood there before the shimmering pool and gazed longingly at the empty balcony and the drawn blind. Oh Lile, how could this happen to us?

* * * * * *

That evening the sun set slowly and the weather felt quite mild. It was a Friday evening, two days before their imminent departure from the country for the UK.

Ibrahim had gone home and Lile Yusuf and Ronke Adams were playing scrabble beside the pool. The two girls were radiant and arguing over the game when one of the housemaids approached with a queer request.

The maid paused in front of Lile and with poor English, "One madam *dey* for parlour. She says she wants to see you. She says her name is Halima Dambaba, daughter of Ambassador Yahaya Buhari."

The two girls could hardly contain their surprise. Finally, Lile Yusuf asked if the girl had come alone or with her husband.

"She come only herself with driver. She says I should tell you that she really wants see you."

"Bring her here", Lile said and as the servant walked away the two girls looked quizzically at each other and shrugged.

"I hope she hasn't come to make trouble," Ronke said and Lile shook her head.

"I don't recall Halima as a trouble maker. Oh, she's really only a kid. Still in her teens."

They looked up as the housemaid led Halima Dambaba to the poolside and Ronke exclaimed in surprise "She's only a baby!"

Halima was dressed in a native female caftan and calf sandals. She looked so young and terribly vulnerable that evening and instantly Ronke felt the pent up hostility inside her melting away as Ibrahim Dambaba's wife approached, clearly shy and scared; a false smile struggled bravely on her face.

Halima stood awkwardly in front of the two girls as the house help left and for a moment the three girls were lost for some initiative. Halima was staring wide eyed at Lile Yusuf, pensive and frightened and then she broke down, she crashed to her knees and held Lile Yusuf's legs, weeping profusely and pleading in both Hausa and English.

"Oh Lile, oh Lile - they forced me to marry him, my parents forced me to marry Ibrahim Dambaba. I couldn't say 'No', I couldn't refuse, they told me you were dead, that some ritualist had kidnapped you - oh Lile, oh Lile forgive me, forgive me…"

And Halima Dambaba wept so heartbrokenly, her tears drenched Lile Yusuf's clothes and Lile and Ronke kept pleading with her to stop crying and take a seat.

Finally, she was persuaded into a chair, still weeping into a tear-soaked handkerchief.

"It's not your fault, Halima," Ronke absolved her. "You are just another innocent victim of our super masculine world where women are treated like toys and property."

Halima stopped sobbing to stare at Ronke. "I don't hate Ibrahim Dambaba. He is my husband. I respect Ibrahim. That is why I have come on his behalf to plead with Lile Yusuf to stop tormenting Ibrahim and making him because Ibrahim is so miserable.

"For the past one week, Ibrahim has not been able to sleep. Each night I hear him crying in his bedroom and I can't help him, I can only cry for him too.

"So I told him I would come and plead with Lile to forgive him and marry him as a second wife. I will concede all the rights of a first wife to Lile Yusuf. After all, I know that Ibrahim Dambaba agreed to marry me only because he believed Lile Yusuf was dead."

It was a peculiar and unbelievable speech and the girl had delivered it with such spontaneous sincerity that it struck home and left her two hosts utterly speechless for a while.

Lile Yusuf looked at Halima, somewhat confused. "You mean you want me to also marry Ibrahim?"

"Yes".

No hesitation.

Halima said, "We are good Muslims. A man can marry as much as four women if he chooses to. I don't want to come between you and Ibrahim."

"My father married only one wife and even after she died he refused to marry another woman."

"But you love Ibrahim and he loves you. I saw some of your letters to him before your accident."

"I loved Ibrahim", Lile said softly. "Maybe I still love him, but I can survive without him.

"Tell Ibrahim Dambaba that if he still values my respect then he must discipline his emotion and forget how he feels about me; let him learn a sense of responsibility and love for the woman who now bears his surname.

"Tell Ibrahim Dambaba that the first lesson life teaches every man is that sometimes you win and sometimes you lose. It is called *kismet.*"

* * * * * *

Halima Dambaba did not stay too long. After she had gone, the two friends kept discussing the strange visit.

"She isn't quite like I had imagined her to be, she looks so brainwashed by Ibrahim."

Lile said gently, "Ibrahim should not have sent her. I felt pity for her. Forced to marry a man who wants another woman."

Ronke confessed. "I had always imagined Halima as one of these prototype Fulani girls. Reserved, shy and without a mind of her own. But she was clearly burning up with passion just now,"

"What you saw in action right now is sheer Ibrahim Dambaba magic. He has a way of bewitching a woman and soon you feel there is nothing you will not do for Ibrahim. I once slapped my father because of Ibrahim Dambaba."

Ronke's jaws dropped. "No! You couldn't have! You slapped an army General!" Ronke stared at Lile with astonishment Lile laughed.

"It was a long time ago, but I slapped M. S. Yusuf because of Ibrahim Dambaba. If I had a gun that day, I would have shot my father for Ibrahim Dambaba. I really loved the bastard and he abandoned me when I needed him most."

CHAPTER THIRTEEN

*D*ear Diary,

Come this time tomorrow I will be on a plane to London. Flying high in the sky, through space and time, at peace with the drifting clouds, Ronke and I, daddy and Hugo too. For me, a chapter would have closed in my life and new vistas will open before me. A vista devoid of anguish, devoid of memory, devoid of despair, a revitalising spectrum devoid of Ibrahim Dambaba and the subtle aftertaste of his betrayal...

Dear Diary, Ibrahim Dambaba is trying to kill me. Why can't he stay away from me? Like an oyster I need time and space to grow an iron shell around the pearl of emotion, for the truth is that I will always love Ibrahim but now, perforce, it must be from a distance.

People say I am being unfair to Ibrahim but neither has Ibrahim been fair to me and I absolutely refuse to accept him on any other terms different from those terms which once compelled my emotions, terms that are now so irretrievably altered and shortchanged. Dear Diary, If I do not crush this feeling for Ibrahim Dambaba then I will forever remain a hostage to this tyranny of wasted emotion. Because I have come to understand that love is like sugar, it's like chocolates and it's a hard drug, it is destructive when indulged in excess. I am so confused, so confused.

Oh, how I love M.S Yusuf. He has quit alcohol and cigarettes. He told me that he made a vow to Allah to foreswear these vices if I should come back to him alive. Now he must keep this sacred vow. But I feel so guilty each time I find him miserably nursing a flat glass of milk or orange juice while his friends boisterously help themselves to choice vodka and Monte Cristo cigars right before his pleading eyes. Yet a vow is a vow and daddy must force himself to break his vice anyway. On my part, I vow to be a hundred time more loving, a hundred time more caring, and a million time worthy to be the daughter for whom he sacrificed so much of himself. You see, for twenty years I virtually had no one else except my father. He stood by me through the difficult years. Through the idiosyncrasies of childhood. Through the early pangs of puberty. Through sunshine and rain, he was always there for me, an inexhaustible fount of strength and inspiration, M.S. Yusuf and I.

Dear Diary, may I recommend amnesia as a laxative for the terrors of memory. How else would I have coped otherwise with these unscrupulous intrusions of the past? How could I have been so unashamedly in love with Ibrahim Dambaba? How could I have so meekly yielded to him so much power over my emotion, over my mind and happiness?

Love is terrible when it breaks. Because images of the past will forever haunt me and I must fly to the land of Limbo to seek refuge for a while. Ronke has even coined a phrase for it: **U. S. A**. - *Ultra Selective Amnesia.*

M.S Yusuf is organising a small shindig, a little farewell party for us this Saturday evening at the Lekki beach. And Doctor and Mrs Adams flew in this morning from Kano to bid us goodbye. Ronke's Aunt Bola and my Aunt, Hajia Hauwawu will also be at the party with their husbands. So also, will Maureen and a few of our friends from LASU. My only dread now is that Ibrahim Dambaba will seize this opportunity to catch me because I don't trust myself with Ibrahim Dambaba. I pray he will be considerate enough not to show up but even if he does I am determined to remain cool, unruffled and indifferent to him. I will not let Ibrahim Dambaba ruin my day. For who knows when I will see Nigeria again.

Dear diary, I am finally concluding this dark chapter of my life. It has not been easy breaking free from the land of Limbo, from the blind horizon of amnesia. And for this feat I acknowledge and indeed dedicate my triumph to the collective love and support of Ronke Adams and Hugo, of Doctor and Mrs Adams, of Doctor Bala and the staff of Intensive Care Hospital Kano, and of course, of the irrepressible Osage.

But especially I dedicate my victory to M.S. Yusuf who is still paying the awesome price for a divine miracle. Thank you, folks, for being there for me in my season of need and despair. May the Glories and Blessings of Allah enrich your lives abundantly. May your lives be filled with the sunshine. Amin.

EPILOGUE

A t Lekki, the evening rays are golden mild and the ocean meets the sky at the horizon in crimson and gold.

The shores of Lekki beach are covered with white sand and dotted with empty seashells of various shades, sizes and beauty.

Coconut trees trail the coastline and a cool sea breeze blows inland from the inscrutable, calm ocean.

In Lekki the ocean sings and again and again waves of frothing water surges up the shoreline in froths of white, inviting fun and play.

For hours Ronke had been mesmerised by the seduction of this beautiful sea and her artistic mind leapt high and ever higher in bounds of freedom and exultation and echoes of praises rose from her soul to the creator of the universe who had created so much beauty.

She stood by the shoreline and the ocean lapped at her bare feet, teasing and playful.

It was Ronke's very first experience of a seaside beach and for her, it was a thrilling novelty, an unforgettable experience, a strain of living poetry.

That Saturday evening the Lekki beach was filled with an incredible number of people, some were swimming and having fun, some were strolling about aimlessly and yet others were congregating in groups under special, staked out palm-frond stands designed for family seclusion.

Apart from the raffia shades, plastic table and chairs were provided in these enclaves and though it came very expensive to rent this shade for some hours yet the General had procured one of the large beach enclaves for their farewell party.

It had been more of a farewell picnic than party and the small CD player had only been playing the General's Dan Maraya Jos CDs and some of Ronke's new lighthouse family CDs.

They were all having fun. Their table was well stocked with canned beverages, ice cream shakes, pastries and different varieties of baked meat and fish. An inviting tray of salad capped the little buffet.

Maureen was there with two of Lile's friends from LASU and after the meal the young people were drawn to the beach for a game of beach ball, leaving their parents to the boring topic of national politics for which Doctor Adams and the General were two equally matched and eager gladiators who refused to concur with each other's opinion while the women laughed at their obduracy.

* * * ** *

Lile had given up her crutches for an aluminium rubber-padded walking cane with arm grips. She was limping only slightly now for her leg, though still in plaster, was almost healed.

Lile stood by the seashore laughing and shouting and trying hard to encourage her friends who had engaged a rival group in a game of beach ball.

Ronke soon dropped off, out of breath and her face shone with perspiration and fun. Ronke flopped down on the sand beside Lile and then proceeded to drag Lile down beside herself.

"Oh that was so much fun, Lile, I can't remember the last time I had so much fun! At first, I was scared I would suffer a crisis and then the game became so serious and I forgot all about myself. But now I feel fatigued."

"Your mummy is watching anxiously."

Ronke raised her hand and waved at Mrs Adams who waved back in apparent relief. Her husband and the General were locked horns in absolute relish, while Alhaji Halilu Abubakar and Ronke's Aunt were acting the part of moderator for the gladiators.

"Mummy is always watching me," Ronke said with a sigh. "I guess raising a sickle cell child will never be an easy task. Do you know I slept in my mother's bed until I got into the university? Even now, whenever my dad travels, we sleep together. She will be so lonely when Hugo and I leave for London."

Lile smiled softly. "You're still in Nigeria Ronke, but already you are becoming homesick."

"I will miss my mummy," Ronke sighed again.

Lile hugged her closer. "Now, let me tell you a secret, mummy's pet. My dad is processing a visa for your mummy asap. She'll join us in London after the New Year.

"The doctors in London are asking that you should be accompanied to London by someone who shares genetic affinity or something like that…" by the time Lile had finished talking, Ronke had pounced ecstatically on top of her and the two girls were laughing and rolling on the beach sand before the amused eyes of their friends.

* * * * * *

The brown Mercedes was parked unobtrusively some distance away from the Generals shack that evening. Inside the car,

Ibrahim Dambaba sat smoking a cigarette and next to him sat his friend Kabiru Buhari.

For two hours the two friends had been watching Lile and her friends playing on the beach. This was Ibrahim's first sight of her since she came back home. And the sight of Lile Yusuf in a leg cast and a walking cane was very painful to him, a reminder of her ordeal and his betrayal while she was fighting for her life.

In the car, Ibrahim remained mostly silent, chain-smoking and lost in his private thought and Kabiru did not want to intrude. Besides, what was there to say? Personally, Kabiru had tried to intercede on Ibrahim's behalf with Lile, drawing on his close association with her, but she rebuffed him, probably even holding him guilty for Ibrahim's marriage to Halima.

And so now Kabiru also kept quiet, watching Lile and her friends having fun on the beach. Personally, Kabiru felt that this was a very painful way Ibrahim had chosen to torture himself for a tragic error of which he was clearly not to blame. A victim of kismet. Plain and simple.

Ibrahim threw away the butt of the spent cigarette and lit another cigarette. The habit was a recent one, one he had picked up during the shocking reality of Lile Yusuf's disappearance. Now he was smoking an average of three packs a day.

Ibrahim glanced at Kabiru casually.

"I'm going to London next month."

"London!"

"What choice have I, Kabiru? What choice?"

* * * * * *

Back at their stand, the young people came back with faces shining with excitement and fun. The time was past seven in the evening and the beach had become cooler, darker, and less noisy for many people had departed.

However, the beach was well lit with multi-coloured bulbs and the enclaves were buzzing with life and merry making all around them.

Ronke had broken the news to her mum and her parents' gratitude to the Genera had been apparent but the General M.S Yusuf had schemed far much more than this.

Before all of them, he proclaimed himself as Ronke's Godfather. Three percent of his Oil Tech stocks would be transferred to Ronke's name and as one of the Company's director, she was being placed on scholarship to further her studies abroad alongside Lile Yusuf in any school of their choice.

Turning to Ronke Adams the General said in his deep baritone.

"I don't have the power to cure you of sickle cell anaemia, only Allah in His supreme majesty can do that. But I want you to know that as from today you will never lack for money or for friends. You gave Lile Yusuf a home when she had no home and above all, you gave her yourself when she needed a friend and a sister.

"Ronke Adams, my family will eternally be grateful to you and your parents here."

"And to Hugo," Hajia Hauwawu chipped in.

"And Hugo too," the General agreed.

And they all clapped their hands spontaneously, laughter and happiness suffused the night with their happy voices and merged with the sounds of the surging ocean as its waves broke at the shoreline into millions of frothing bubbles of light.

Made in the USA
Middletown, DE
22 November 2022

15816866R00066